Monster Mountain

Thunderbelle's Bad Mood

For Djazia Spowers
K.W.
For Ella and Marcie, with love
G.P-R.

First published in 2007 by Orchard Books
First paperback publication in 2008

ORCHARD BOOKS
338 Euston Road, London NW1 3BH
Orchard Books Australia
Level 17/207 Kent St, Sydney, NSW 2000

ISBN 978 1 84362 621 3 (hardback)
ISBN 978 1 84362 629 9 (paperback)

1 3 5 7 9 10 8 6 4 2 (hardback)
1 3 5 7 9 10 8 6 4 2 (paperback)

Printed in China

Orchard Books is a division of Hachette Children's Books,
an Hachette Livre UK company.

www.orchardbooks.co.uk

Monster Mountain

Thunderbelle's Bad Mood

Karen Wallace

Illustrated by

Guy Parker-Rees

ORCHARD BOOKS

One day Thunderbelle woke up.
She was in a really bad mood.
Nothing was right.

The sky was too blue. The sun was
too yellow. The grass was too
green. Thunderbelle stamped her
feet on the floor.

The other monsters did not know
what to do. They listened to the
terrible noise.

"What is going on?" said Roxorus.

"Why is Thunderbelle so cross?"
said Clodbuster.

Mudmighty shook his head.

"I do not know," he said.

"I do!" squawked Pipsquawk.
She peeped through
Thunderbelle's window.

"What is wrong?" asked Pipsquawk.
"Nothing!" shouted Thunderbelle.
"Go away!"

The other monsters wanted
Thunderbelle to feel better.
But when they tried to talk to her
she would not reply.
"Thunderbelle is in a bad mood,"
said Pipsquawk in a loud whisper.

So Roxorus went to
clean out his cave.

Clodbuster went to
build his new house.

And Mudmighty
went to dig
up his garden.

10

Then Pipsquawk had a brilliant
idea! She rang the Brilliant Ideas
gong as loud she could.

Bong!

Bong!

Bong!

The other monsters ran over.
Even Thunderbelle came. But
she was still in a bad mood.
"What is your brilliant idea?"
said Thunderbelle crossly.

"It is a way to make your bad mood disappear," said Pipsquawk. "When I am in a temper I flap my wings really hard and then I feel better."

"So what?" said Thunderbelle. "I do not have wings."

"When I am in a bad temper I dig a deep hole," said Mudmighty. "It always makes me feel better." Thunderbelle pulled a face. "I do not like digging," she said.

Roxorus took Thunderbelle's arm.
"Come skateboarding! We'll go so
fast you'll forget your bad mood."
But Thunderbelle pulled away and
looked even more cross.

"I know what to do!" cried Clodbuster. "I will lend you my big hammer so you can bang nails into some wood. That always works."

"It will not work for me!" shouted
Thunderbelle. And she stamped her
foot in a big puddle. SPLAT!
Thunderbelle was muddy from her
head to her feet.
"Yuck!" she cried. "I hate mud!"

The other monsters knew
Thunderbelle was being silly. But
they didn't want to laugh at her. It
would only make her more cross.

But it was too late.
A giggle shook
Clodbuster's
shoulders.

Roxorus grinned
before he could
stop himself.

Mudmighty put
his hand over his
mouth. A loud
chuckle came
through his fingers.

Thunderbelle was so angry, she threw herself down in the puddle and howled.

"Oh dear," squawked Pipsquawk. "Oh dear, oh dear, oh dear."

Then Pipsquawk had another
brilliant idea. "Follow me!" she
cried and flew off through
the trees.

Poor Thunderbelle!
She was so muddy, she could not
see in front of her.

So Clodbuster took one arm.
And Roxorus took the other.
And Mudmighty made sure there
were no rocks to fall over.

Pipsquawk led them down the side
of Monster Mountain.

At last she came to a big wide
river. The water was bright blue
and bubbly. It looked wonderful!

Pipsquawk flew onto
Thunderbelle's shoulder.
"Jump in!" she squawked.
"You'll feel absolutely fantastic!"

For the first time that day
Thunderbelle did as she was told.
Pipsquawk was right. The water
felt cool and lovely.

Soon Thunderbelle was clean again.
And there was a big smile on her
face. Thunderbelle's bad mood had
gone away!

"I have something to say!"
cried Thunderbelle.
"What is that?" shouted the
other monsters.

Thunderbelle clapped her hands. "Next time I feel cross, I shall jump into the river and have a bath!"

Thunderbelle laughed and splashed as hard as she could. And very soon, all her friends were playing in the water, too!

All priced at £4.99. Monster Mountain books are available from
all good bookshops, or can be ordered direct from the publisher:
Orchard Books, PO BOX 29, Douglas IM99 1BQ. Credit card orders
please telephone 01624 836000 or fax 01624 837033 or visit our website:
www.orchardbooks.co.uk or e-mail: bookshop@enterprise.net for details.

To order please quote title, author and ISBN and your full name and address.
Cheques and postal orders should be made payable to 'Bookpost plc.'
Postage and packing is FREE within the UK
(overseas customers should add £2.00 per book).

Prices and availability are subject to change.